Down Girl and Sit

Home on the Range

Down Girl and Sit

Home on the Range

by Lucy Nolan

Illustrations by Mike Reed

Marshall Cavendish Children

Marshall Cavendish Corporation
99 White Plains Road
Tarrytown, NY 10591
www.marshallcavendish.us/kids

Library of Congress Cataloging-in-Publication Data

Nolan, Lucy A.
Home on the range / by Lucy Nolan ; illustrated by Mike Reed. — 1st ed.
p. cm. — (Down Girl and Sit)
Summary: Dogs Down Girl and Sit accompany their masters to a dude ranch,
where they encounter scary "squirrels" that live in holes in the ground, stampedes,
and enemies even worse than their nemesis, the cat that lives next door.
ISBN 978-0-7614-5649-0
[1. Dogs—Fiction. 2. Dude ranches—Fiction. 3. Humorous stories.] I.
Reed, Mike, 1951- ill. II. Title.
PZ7.N688Ho 2010
[Fic]—dc22
2009005958

The illustrations were created in Corel Painter 8.

Book design by Adam Mietlowski

Printed in China (E)

Marshall Cavendish Chapter Book, First edition

1 3 5 6 4 2

Marshall Cavendish
Children

Contents

Hamburger Man's house

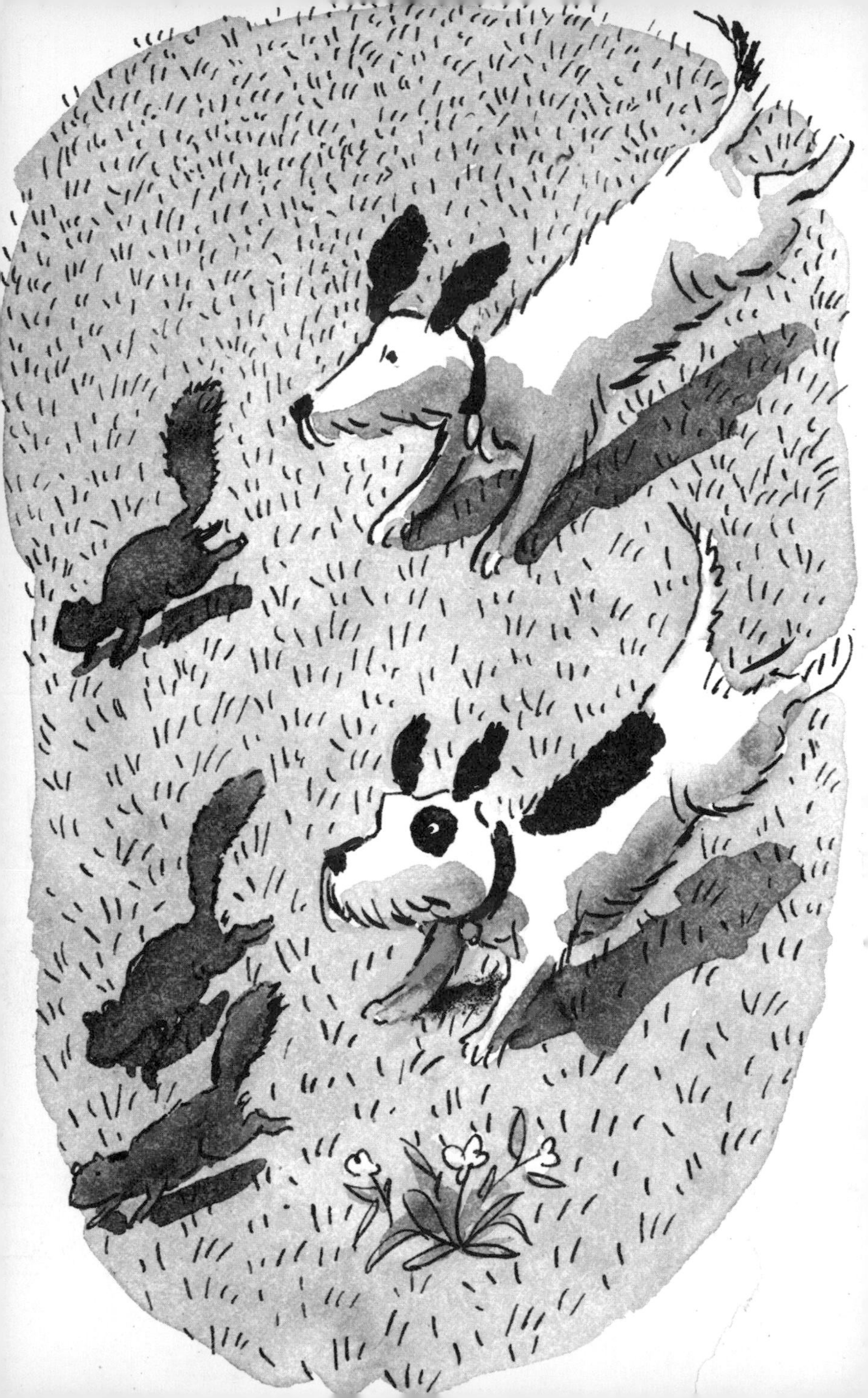

Chapter 1

Don't Fence Me In

Hi there. My name is Down Girl.

I am a very busy dog. I spend most of my time chasing squirrels.

I know what you're thinking. You're thinking that I lead the most exciting life ever. But dogs are meant for so much more.

Oh, sure, we chase cats, too. But that is not what I'm talking about.

Here's the truth about dogs. Our worst enemy is not a squirrel or a cat. Our worst enemy is a fence.

In our neighborhood, we have a saying: A fence keeps a dog on one side and excitement on the other. Dogs could rule the world if there weren't any fences.

Sit is my best friend and neighbor. She understands how special dogs are. She also understands how rotten cats are.

A very rotten cat lives behind us. His name is Here Kitty Kitty. He likes to sit on the fence and tease us.

"One day I'm coming over that fence," I say. "And then you'll be in big trouble."

Here Kitty Kitty just yawns. He does that when he's scared.

My master, Rruff, can leave the yard anytime he wants. Sometimes he takes me with him. Whenever we leave the yard, we always have an adventure. Last week, we went on a trip I'll never forget.

I watched very closely when Rruff started packing the car. He didn't pack towels, so I knew we weren't going to the beach. He didn't pack a tent, so I knew we weren't going camping. Aha! He put a bag on the front seat.

I climbed up to see what was inside. Doughnuts! That must mean . . .

Oh, you can't tell anything by that. He packs doughnuts everywhere we go.

"Down, girl!" Rruff called.

How sweet. He wanted to make sure he packed me, too!

"Rruff!" I answered.

I still didn't know where we were going, but that was okay. I like surprises. And there was another surprise, too. Sit and her master were going with us!

We climbed into our seats and set off. We drove for two days.

Sit and I love our masters. We really do. But if you want to find out how annoying someone is, just take a long car ride with them.

Rruff and Sit's master didn't want us to sing along with the radio. When we stopped for breaks, they didn't want to sniff the interesting motorcycle men with us. And when we had picnics, they never wanted to crawl under the other tables. Or stick their heads into strange picnic baskets.

It is hard to have an adventure with people who have very tiny imaginations.

The farther we drove, the more things changed outside the windows. The land got very flat, and there were lots of wide-open spaces. We could chase cats and squirrels for hours out there!

Finally, we turned up a long, dusty driveway. We couldn't wait to get out of the car. It was time for our adventure to begin!

Chapter 2

City Dogs

As soon as our masters opened the doors, we set off exploring. A scruffy old dog came out to greet us.

"Howdy, city dogs," he said. "Welcome to Cowpoke Dude Ranch."

City dogs?!

I didn't like the sound of that. Did he think we sleep on soft pillows? And ride around in air-conditioned cars? And have our food handed to us in a bowl?

Sit and I looked at each other.

Ack!

We *are* city dogs.

"My name's Git Along," the dog said. "Who are you?"

Sit and I introduced ourselves. Then we all sniffed one another. It was the polite thing to do.

"Why, you two smell as pretty as a speckled pup in a field of daisies," Git Along said. "But I think we can fix that."

He turned and trotted away. "Come on, let's mosey over to the barn and find something to roll in."

Sit and I weren't sure how to mosey. So we just trotted along behind him.

As we followed him along the fence, we heard footsteps coming up alongside us. They were kind of loud. Must be a Labrador retriever.

Sit and I turned around. Whoa! That thing was no Labrador retriever!

"What is that?" I asked.

"That rascal is a horse," Git Along said.

He sounded pretty calm about it. He didn't even try to chase it up a tree.

We stood outside the horse's yard and watched as the big animal pawed the ground and snickered. I was beginning to

think Here Kitty Kitty didn't look so bad.

A man was talking to the horse. Then he suddenly jumped on the horse's back!

"Nice try, fella," I thought, "but you'll never wrestle that thing to the ground."

Suddenly, the horse ran through the gate and thundered away. And the man was still on his back!

"Did you see that?" I asked Sit.

But Sit was already halfway to the barn.

I trotted after Sit. On the other side of the barn, we saw a pretty white fence. Ah, I was wondering where Git Along lived. That must be his yard right there.

Now, this was my kind of fence. There was plenty of space beneath it. Git Along could come and go as he pleased. It made me wonder what the point of it was.

I crawled under the boards to have a look. Git Along's yard was nice enough, but it was much smaller than my yard. And honestly, it was really kind of boring. There weren't any bird feeders or sticks or anything.

Snort!

I felt a burst of hot breath by my ear.

I was beginning to think this wasn't Git Along's yard after all. I turned around and found myself staring into two big, hairy nostrils!

"Snort!" the nostrils said again. They were not happy.

I shot under the fence just before the giant nostrils charged. It was a good thing, because two giant horns followed right behind. Sit's eyes were wide, but Git Along's eyes were even wider.

"You've got gumption, City Dog," said Git Along. "I've never gone under that fence myself."

"Really?" I asked.

"No way," Git Along said. "Around here, we have a saying about fences."

"What's that?" I asked.

Git Along smiled.

"A good fence keeps a dog on one side and excitement on the other."

Chapter 3

Varmints

Sit and I really liked this ranch. There was nothing but sky as far as the eye could see. And here's the best part. There were hardly any trees.

Now, that is very important. I will tell you why. If there are no trees, there are no squirrels!

It was nice to be on vacation from squirrels. We didn't have to get cricks in our necks from looking up all the time. We could trot along, watching the ground for a change.

"Look at me!" Sit said. She trotted backward, looking down.

"I can't see you," I said. "I'm looking down, too!"

We trotted forward, we trotted backward, we trotted sideways.

We trotted right into each other.

We did look up once when we heard something rumbling in the distance. It was big and black and had long, pointy horns in front. "Is that a bull?" I asked.

"I think it's a truck," Sit said.

"But it has horns," I argued.

"Trucks have horns," Sit reminded me.

It did kind of smell like gasoline, but I wasn't totally convinced.

Sit and I trotted away from the barn and the cabins and the ranch house. The yard got rocky and scraggly. I would never say this to Git Along, but they could sure use a nice lawn out there. A couple of flowerpots wouldn't hurt, either.

As we walked along, I saw a hole. Git Along must have started it and forgot about it. I would finish it for him.

I leaned down to look inside and—whoa! What was that?!

A squirrel popped out of the hole. It twitched its nose at me, and then—I am not lying—it barked at me!

Then it popped back down into the hole.

"Did a squirrel just come out of that hole?" I asked. "And did he just bark at me?"

"I'm afraid so," Sit said.

"Why would a squirrel do that?" I asked.

Sit grinned. "Maybe he thinks you're nuts!"

This was no time for jokes! Sit and I dove toward the hole and started digging.

"He had huge, beady eyes," I said. "And big, ugly toenails."

Sit stopped digging. "So why are we going after him?"

"He barked at me," I reminded her. "I can't forgive a squirrel who barked at me!"

But wait! While we were digging in one hole, the squirrel popped up out of another one.

What kind of crazy squirrel was this?

I sat down on the first hole, and Sit sat down on the second. We had the squirrel trapped now.

But wait! The squirrel popped up from a third hole.

Sit and I ran from hole to hole and barked. That squirrel popped up all over the place.

He popped up to our left. Then to our right. Then in front of us. Then behind us.

We finally had to face the facts.

"I think we're dealing with a whole bunch of squirrels," I said.

"I don't know," Sit said. "Maybe it's just one squirrel, but he's twice as smart as we are."

Nah!

"If we dig deep enough, I bet we can run around down there," I said.

I liked the thought of that, so I dug even faster. Sit started a new hole a few feet away.

I dug down for awhile. Then the tunnel went sideways.

"I hear something," I said.

"I hear something, too!" Sit said.

I kept digging. Sit kept digging.

"I think I see something," I said.

"I think I see something, too!" Sit said.

I kept digging. Sit kept digging.

"I smell bad breath," I said.

"I smell even worse breath!" Sit said.

There was silence.

"Sit, is that you?"

Another pause. "Yes, is that you?"

"Yes."

More silence.

"Sit, are we stuck?"

"I'm afraid so."

There we were, wedged tight in a squirrel tunnel. Could things get any worse?

Well, as a matter of fact, yes.

Just as we were discussing the best way to get out, a squirrel barked in my ear. It scared me to death.

I jumped into the air. Or, at least, my

back feet jumped into the air. The rest of
me was stuck in the tunnel—with a lunatic
squirrel.

I wriggled and wriggled until I was
able to back out.

Git Along showed up just then.

"Wow, you went down the varmint
hole?" he asked. "I've never done that
before."

I was surprised. "You haven't?"

"No, I was afraid I'd get stuck tighter than a cocklebur in a collie's fur."

The whole way back to the ranch, we kept our heads down, looking for those squirrels. We could get cricks in our necks from that.

We found Rruff and Sit's master at the evening cookout. They were trying to impress some cowgirls by playing their guitars. Our masters had bandannas tied around their necks. They looked just like

those dogs that catch Frisbees at the park.

Sit and I sat with Git Along by the campfire. He wanted to hear all about our adventure.

"Squirrels? That's not what we call those varmints," he said. "Out here we call them prairie dogs."

"Because they bark?" I asked.

"Exactly," Git along said. "There are lots of animals that wish they were dogs."

"Well, who doesn't know that?" Sit asked.

Git Along thought a little longer.

"You say your squirrels climb trees?" he asked.

I nodded.

"You mean, they can drop out of the sky without warning?" he asked.

"Yep," I said.

"Wow," Git Along said.

As the stars twinkled and the fire crackled, Sit and Git Along and I exchanged campfire stories about squirrels.

"You know what?" Git Along finally said. "You two are all right for city dogs."

You know what? We agreed.

When the campfire died down, our masters said good-bye to the cowgirls and walked away. Sit and I followed them. We couldn't wait to see where we'd be sleeping.

As it turns out, we were staying in a cabin. There was a rug for us to lie on. And TV. And air-conditioning.

"This is no way to have an adventure!" I said. "We should be sleeping under the stars."

"Yeah, with the prairie dogs," Sit agreed.

We looked at each other, then looked out the door.

"You know, we could protect our masters better if we stayed inside," I said.

"We should do what's best for them," Sit agreed.

So we protected our masters the best way we knew how.

We slept under their beds.

Chapter 4

Stampede

The next morning, Git Along announced that we were going on a cattle drive.

"We're going to move the cows from here to there," Git Along explained. He nodded across a wide-open space. It was kind of hard to tell where "there" was.

Now, this was a bad idea for a lot of reasons.

For one thing, the cows weren't on leashes. And for another thing, there were a whole bunch of them and not many of us. This made me very nervous.

We walked beside the cows, but our masters got up on horses. It was not a pretty sight.

We walked and stopped and walked and stopped. It was taking an awfully long time.

"Why are we doing this?" I finally asked. Git Along didn't have a good answer.

"It makes about as much sense as putting pants on a possum," he agreed. Git Along nodded toward a wagon being pulled by horses.

"Ignore everything else," he said. "Just keep your eyes on that."

"What is it?" I asked.

"That's the chuck wagon," Git Along said. "It's like a food dish on wheels."

That's all Git Along had to tell us. We kept our eyes on the chuck wagon all day.

Git Along was right. The chuck wagon was filled with treats. It had sausage. And beans. And biscuits. Every now and then, the cook would throw us some food.

That night, we gathered around the campfire again. Our masters were sitting with the cowgirls, so Sit and I moseyed over to Git Along. We sang songs together and sneaked bad coffee.

In the distance, we could hear howling.

"Oh, good grief," I said. "Someone please tell those prairie dogs to be quiet."

"Those are coyotes," Git Along explained. "They want to be dogs, too, but they're not. If you see one, don't remind him. It might embarrass him."

The next morning, we started walking again.

Now, don't get me wrong. I liked being out in the fresh air with my friends and my master. But I just didn't see the point of it. Couldn't we go from here to there without the cows? They were really slowing us down.

"Is there a way to hurry this up?" I asked when we stopped for lunch. "Can't the cows run?"

"No, that would be a stampede," Git Along said. "Stampedes are dangerous. Those cows get crazier than a bunch of jackrabbits trying to outrun a flea. They'd trample everything in their way."

Oh, well.

Sit and I stayed near the chuck wagon. Or better yet, we sat *in* the chuck wagon.

When we climbed in, we saw that most of the food was in cans. Dogs can't do anything with cans.

But wait! There was a bag.

"What's in it?" Sit asked.

"It doesn't matter," I reminded her. To a dog, one bag of food is worth a thousand cans.

I pulled the bag off the shelf.

"Git along!" the cook shouted.

He must not see very well. I didn't look a thing like Git Along.

We jumped out of the wagon and took the bag behind a rock.

Up until then, I hadn't been thrilled about this cattle drive. But I must admit, there's nothing like eating an entire bag of white bread under a warm western sun.

Before long, it was time to start walking and stopping again. It took a couple of hours.

Then, in the late afternoon, I saw something in the distance. Was it a rock? Or was it a prairie dog?

I barked, so Sit barked. I started jumping. Sit started jumping.

The cows looked up and started to moo. I didn't realize cows were so scared of prairie dogs. Or maybe rocks.

We barked and jumped. We ran around. Suddenly, the cows started running, too.

In seconds, everything was out of control.

There was dust. There were cows. There was barking. There was shouting. There were hooves. There were nostrils. There was mooing.

If we didn't stop them, the cows were going to stir up the prairie dogs. And if the prairie dogs started stampeding, we could have a real disaster on our hands.

The cows knocked over some bushes. They trampled Rruff's hat. But when they tried to run over the chuck wagon, we decided they had gone too far.

Sit and I ran toward them. The cows turned. We chased them right back the way we had come.

I didn't know cows could move that fast. It sure would be easier if they would do this all the time.

Finally, when the dust settled, we realized we were back at the ranch—right where we had started.

The good news was, we had saved the chuck wagon. The bad news was, it was still out there where we had left it.

That night, we sat around a campfire outside the ranch house and ate frozen pizza.

Rruff and Sit's master didn't look too happy, but maybe they were just tired. They slept awfully well. I, on the other hand, didn't sleep a wink.

We had escaped danger once that day. I didn't think the cows would cause us any more trouble. But if those prairie dogs decided to stampede during the night, we might not be so lucky again.

Chapter 5

Ugly Dogs

The next morning, we were back on the trail. It seemed that we were going to take those cows right back to where they had already been.

Hanging back with the cows was cramping my style. Sit and I decided to go off on our own for awhile.

"Let's just walk to the fence and back," I said.

Sit looked doubtfully toward the horizon.

"Are you sure there's a fence?" she asked.

"Do you really think they'd have all these cows off their leashes if there was no fence?" I asked.

"Good point," Sit said.

We struck out across the range. The feeling of freedom was incredible. We were free to run as far and as fast as we wanted. We were free to wallow in the dust. We could live the life of adventure we were meant to lead.

"I'm as happy as a hop toad in a hoot owl tree!" Sit said.

"What does that mean?" I asked.

"I have no idea," Sit said.

"Onward to the fence!" we cried.

We kept going. And going. And going. And going.

And going.

When it started getting dark, we finally had to face facts.

"There's no fence, is there?" I asked.

"I'm afraid not," Sit said.

As the evening grew cooler and darker, Sit and I huddled together. We were out on

the range alone. No, that wasn't quite true. We were out there alone except for the really big, really pointy lizard that was staring at us.

Then the coyotes started to howl. First one howled. Then another. Then another.

It hadn't seemed so bad when we were sitting around the campfire with our masters. But now those coyotes sounded downright scary.

Then we realized something even scarier.

Nobody was going to feed us.

"Maybe we could eat that lizard," I suggested.

"I don't know," Sit said. "That lizard looks like something that could eat *us*."

As the moon rose, we knew we wouldn't see our masters again until morning. That is, if we ever saw them again.

"Down Girl?" Sit asked. "Would you call this an adventure?"

"Yes, I think I would," I said.

"I don't like adventures after all," Sit said.

When morning came, things didn't look any better. The wide-open spaces we had loved the day before now looked big and empty.

Just when we were sure we would never see our masters again, we saw a dog. It was the ugliest dog we had ever seen. But at least we must be near a house.

"Hi," I said. "Do you live around here?"

The ugly dog didn't answer. He just stared at me.

"Can you tell us how to get back to Git Along's house?" Sit asked.

Now the ugly dog stared at Sit.

"Are you out here by yourself?" I asked.

"If you are, you need to be careful of the coyotes," Sit warned.

The ugly dog just blinked.

"Coyotes are embarrassed they're not dogs," I added.

The ugly dog turned around and loped off. We followed behind him.

"Hey, wait!" Sit called. "Can you give us directions back to the cows?"

"And maybe a doughnut?" I added.

The ugly dog didn't want to have anything to do with us. How rude!

He trotted faster. We trotted faster.

"It doesn't have to be a doughnut," I called. "It could be toast."

The ugly dog started running. We started running, too.

"You don't even have to butter it!" I said.

The ugly dog ran behind a rock. We ran behind a rock.

The ugly dog turned and growled at us.

I have been growled at before by a cranky wiener dog. And I have been barked at by a squirrel. But somehow, this seemed much worse.

The ugly dog stared at us. We stared at him.

Then another ugly dog appeared. And then an even uglier one.

Now, there comes a time in every dog's life when she either has to be brave and stand her ground or run away with her tail tucked between her legs.

We ran.

The ugly dogs ran after us.

They yipped and snapped. And unfortunately, they could run as fast as we could.

Just when I thought we were goners, we found the one thing that moved faster than the ugly dogs.

A gasoline-powered bull.

When that thing came roaring toward us, the ugly dogs took off. Sit and I would have, too, but we heard Git Along calling to us.

Git Along hopped out of the back of the bull. Okay, so maybe it was a truck after all. Our masters got out.

We were so thrilled to see them, we jumped all over them. Then we kissed them on the lips.

"Down, girl!" "Sit!"

They were happy to see us, too. It's nice to be loved.

We climbed into the back of the truck, and Git Along nodded toward the distance.

"You were playing with coyotes?" he asked. "I've always been afraid to do that."

About all we could see of the coyotes then were their ugly, bushy tails.

"Well, no wonder they're embarrassed," I thought.

The truck turned and headed back. We passed the cows and just kept going.

I stretched out in the back of the truck. "Ah, now this is my kind of cattle drive!"

We were heading back to the cabin. To our rug. And TV. And air-conditioning.

Sit didn't have it quite right about adventures. We *do* like adventures.

But we like them even better when they're over.

Chapter 6

The Trail Home

The next morning, it was time to head home.

"I'm going to miss this place," I said.

"It's going to be quieter than a moth on a buttermilk biscuit without you," Git Along said.

Sit and I climbed into the car with our masters. Soon we were rolling down the highway.

Before long, the sky would get smaller. Fences would start appearing again. But that was okay. It would mean we were getting closer to home.

53

We enjoyed the ranch, but let's face it. Things are not normal there.

At home, if something looks like a dog, it is a dog. Lizards aren't all scary looking. And squirrels are up high in the trees, where they belong. They don't pop out of holes when you're not expecting it.

Of course, we would still have to deal with Here Kitty Kitty when we got home. But we were kind of looking forward to that.

And that's when we realized something very important about fences. You can say what you will about them, but they always give you something to look forward to.

You see, when you're on one side of a fence, there's always something waiting on the other side.

Sometimes it's a cat.

Sometimes it's big, hairy nostrils.

And sometimes, just sometimes, it's the biggest adventure of your life.